# Contents

# A Note About This Story

**The time:** 1625
**The place:** France

In 1625, a young man called D'Artagnan comes to Paris. D'Artagnan wants to be a King's musketeer. Musketeers are special soldiers. Some musketeers work for King Louis and some work for Cardinal Richelieu. The King's musketeers do not like the cardinal's musketeers. Sometimes they fight each other.

D'Artagnan is friends with three of the King's musketeers. Their names are Athos, Aramis and Porthos. Monsieur de Treville is the captain of the King's musketeers.

At this time there are problems between England and France. People think there will be a war. Cardinal Richelieu is a powerful man. He is very close to King Louis. The cardinal does not like the English.

D'Artagnan is in love with a pretty young girl called Constance. Constance is Queen Anne's maid.

Queen Anne is from Austria. She is married to King Louis but they are not happy. Anne is secretly in love with an English man – the Duke of Buckingham. The Queen gives the Duke of Buckingham some diamonds. The diamonds were a present from the King to the Queen. Buckingham takes the diamonds back to London. But the cardinal knows about the diamonds. The cardinal wants to stop the Queen and Buckingham's love.

ALEXANDRE DUMAS

# The Three Musketeers

Retold by Nicholas Murgatroyd

**MACMILLAN**

## BEGINNER LEVEL

*Founding Editor:* John Milne

The Macmillan Readers provide a choice of enjoyable reading materials for learners of English. The series is published at six levels – Starter, Beginner, Elementary, Pre-intermediate, Intermediate and Upper.

## Level Control

Information, structure and vocabulary are controlled to suit the students' ability at each level.

## The number of words at each level:

| | |
|---|---|
| Starter | about 300 basic words |
| Beginner | about 600 basic words |
| Elementary | about 1100 basic words |
| Pre-intermediate | about 1400 basic words |
| Intermediate | about 1600 basic words |
| Upper | about 2200 basic words |

## Answer Keys

An answer key for the *Exercises* section can be found at www.macmillanenglish.com/readers

## Audio Download

There is an audio download available for this title.
Visit www.macmillanenglish.com/readers for more information.

# A Note About The Author

Alexandre Dumas was born on 24th July 1802 in Villers-Cotteret, a town in northern France. His father was a soldier in Napoleon's army. His father died when Dumas was four years old. Dumas' mother was poor, so he could not go to school. But Dumas read a lot of books and he liked telling stories.

At the age of twenty, Dumas moved to Paris. He worked for the Duc D'Orleans, who later became King of France. Dumas wrote historical plays and novels. His most famous are *The Three Musketeers*, *The Man in the Iron Mask* and *The Count of Monte Cristo*. People liked his stories because they were very exciting. Dumas became rich and famous. He liked eating and drinking. He also liked beautiful women. Dumas had four children. His oldest son's name was Alexandre. He became a writer too.

In 1851, Dumas moved to Brussels in Belgium. After Belgium, he lived in Russia for two years. His books were very popular in Russia because many Russians spoke French. Dumas was very happy there. Later he moved to Italy and started a newspaper there. Finally, he returned to Paris in 1864. He died on the 5th of December 1870 in Puys in northen France. His body now lies next to Victor Hugo and Voltaire in Paris. Many of his books are now films.

# The People In This Story

D'Artagnan

Athos

Aramis

Porthos

Constance

Milady

Cardinal Richelieu

Rochefort

The Duke of Buckingham

Queen Anne

The King

de Winter

Planchet

Monsieur de Treville

Felton

Grimaud

# A Picture Dictionary

Sword

Castle

Ladder

Horse

Carriage

Glove

Gun

Nun

Convent

Inn

Cellar

Innkeeper

Ring

Bag of gold

Diamonds

Ship

Boat

Port

# 1

# Diamonds and Gold

It was April 1625. Queen Anne of France was in her bedroom with her maid, Constance. The Queen was very unhappy. The King wanted her to wear some diamonds at a dance. The diamonds were a present to the Queen from the King. The dance was in two weeks' time.

'I cannot wear the diamonds. I gave them to the Duke of Buckingham,' Anne told Constance. 'But now the Duke is in England. The King will be very angry.'

The Queen started to cry. Constance knew the Queen was right. The diamonds were a big problem.

Then Constance had an idea. 'Madam,' she said. 'I know someone who can help you.'

'Really? Who?' asked the Queen.

'I have a friend,' Constance replied. 'His name is D'Artagnan. He is the bravest man in France.'

'Oh Constance! Go and ask him now,' the Queen said. 'I hope he can do it. I will give him a lot of money. But tell him it must be a secret.'

'I will, Madam,' Constance said. She left the palace and ran to D'Artagnan's home. She knocked on the door.

'Hello?' D'Artagnan shouted. 'Who is it?'

'It's me, Constance,' she replied. D'Artagnan opened the door. D'Artagnan was a young man who wanted to be a musketeer in the King's army. He was brave and handsome. He was in love with Constance.

'My darling!' D'Artagnan said. He tried to kiss Constance, but she stopped him. Constance was very pretty and she loved D'Artagnan. But the Queen was in danger. The diamonds were the most important thing now.

'Not now D'Artagnan,' Constance said. 'Please … you must help me.'

'How can I help you, my darling?' D'Artagnan asked. 'You know I will do anything for you.'

'You must keep it a secret,' Constance said.

'Of course I'll keep it a secret, my love,' replied D'Artagnan. 'Please tell me what it is.'

'You must go to England, D'Artagnan.'

'To England?'

'Yes,' Constance replied. 'You must find the Duke of Buckingham. Ask him for the Queen's diamonds. She needs them back.'

'But how can I go to England?' D'Artagnan asked. 'I haven't got any money.'

'Here, take this,' Constance said. She gave him a small bag. The bag was full of gold.

'But remember,' Constance said. 'This is a secret. Don't tell anyone. The King must not know about the diamonds.'

9

'I promise, my darling,' D'Artagnan said.

'You must be careful,' Constance said. 'There are many people who don't like the Queen or Buckingham. They will try to stop you. Please come back alive, my love.'

Constance kissed him quickly, and then she left. D'Artagnan was very happy. Constance loved him and the Queen wanted him to do something important. He had to go to England immediately. But first he had to visit his friends, the three musketeers. Their names were Porthos, Aramis and Athos.

## 2

# The Journey to Calais

Aramis and Porthos were at Athos's house. They were very bored. There were no wars. They did not have much money because there was no fighting.

Then D'Artagnan arrived with his servant, Planchet. He was very excited.

'Hello!' the three men said. 'Why are you so excited?'

'I can't tell you,' D'Artagnan said. 'It's a secret. I've come to say goodbye.'

'Goodbye? Where are you going?' Athos asked.

'I'm going to England,' D'Artagnan replied. 'Someone needs my help. I must get to Calais tonight. But it will be dangerous. There are people who will try to stop me.'

'We must come with you,' Aramis said.

'But I can't tell you the secret,' D'Artagnan said.

'That's not important,' Aramis replied. 'You know the musketeer's motto: "All for one, and one for all!" Four men will be stronger than one.'

'No, Aramis. We can't go,' Porthos said.

'Why not?' Aramis asked.

'Because we haven't got any money,' Porthos said. 'How can we buy horses?'

'But money isn't a problem,' D'Artagnan replied. And he showed his friends the bag of gold.

'Hooray!' the musketeers shouted. 'All for one, and one for all!'

The next morning they left Athos' house. First they bought eight horses. There were four horses for D'Artagnan and the three musketeers. There were four more horses for their servants.

The four friends left Paris at two o'clock in the morning. The next morning they had breakfast at an inn. There was another traveller in the inn. The traveller saw D'Artagnan and his three friends. He saw they were from the King's musketeers. Then the traveller said loudly,

'The cardinal is the best man in France.'

'My friend,' Porthos replied. 'You must be very stupid. The best man in France is the King.'

'Don't call me stupid,' the traveller shouted.

11

'Then don't say that the cardinal is a better man than the King,' Porthos replied.

Suddenly, the man and Porthos started fighting. D'Artagnan, Athos and Aramis wanted to help but they were in a hurry. There was not enough time. They decided to leave Porthos at the inn.

'Now we are seven,' D'Artagnan said.

Two hours later they saw some men working in the road. The musketeers tried to pass. Suddenly the men pulled out some guns.

'Give us your money, now!' the men shouted. There was a fight and one of the men shot Aramis in the arm.

D'Artagnan, Athos and Aramis rode away quickly but Aramis was very hurt. Soon they had to stop.

'I can't go to Calais like this,' Aramis said. 'I am bleeding. I must stay here.'

Aramis and Porthos's two servants stayed with Aramis. Now only Athos, D'Artagnan and their servants were left. That night Athos and D'Artagnan slept at an inn near Amiens.

The next morning, Athos tried to pay the bill. But the innkeeper was not happy.

'This isn't real money,' he said.

Athos was very angry. 'Of course it's real money. I am not a thief!' he shouted.

Suddenly four strange men entered the room. They were big and they did not look friendly. The men moved towards Athos. Athos knew something was wrong. The men wanted to stop Athos and D'Artagnan. They did not want them to go to England!

'Run!' Athos shouted to D'Artagnan. D'Artagnan and Planchet quickly got on their horses and left the inn.

'What will happen to Athos?' Planchet asked.

'I don't know,' D'Artagnan replied. 'But someone doesn't want us to go to England!'

## 3

# The Duke of Buckingham

The next day D'Artagnan and Planchet came to the port of Calais. They went straight to the boats. A man and his servant stood in front of them. The man spoke to the captain of one of the boats.

'I need to go to England,' the man said.

'That's not possible,' the captain replied. 'You cannot leave France. You must have the cardinal's permission.'

'But I have the cardinal's permission,' the man replied. And he showed the captain a piece of paper.

'Then you must show it to the governor,' replied the captain. 'He lives in that house on the hill,'

What could D'Artagnan do? He did not have permission from the cardinal. But he had to get to England.

D'Artagnan followed the man to the governor's house. The man and his servant went inside the house. They came out ten minutes later. D'Artagnan waited outside.

'Give me that piece of paper,' he said to the man.

'No,' the man replied. 'I need it to go to England.'

'Sir, I must have that piece of paper. Please give it to me,' D'Artagnan said again.

'I will not give you anything,' the man said.

'Then I am very sorry,' D'Artagnan said.

'Why are you sorry?' the man asked.

'For *this*,' D'Artagnan replied, and he cut the man with his sword. He cut him three times. Once for Athos. Once for Porthos. And once for Aramis.

The man's servant tried to stop D'Artagnan, but Planchet cut him too. Now both men were on the floor. They were not moving.

D'Artagnan took the paper from the man's pocket. It read:

*I give permission for this man to go to England.*
                                                    *Cardinal Richelieu*

D'Artagnan took the paper to the captain.

'Can you take me to England,' he asked.

'Yes, I can,' the captain replied. 'But another man is going to England too. We must wait for him.'

'I saw him a few moments ago,' D'Artagnan said. 'He changed his mind. He doesn't want to go to England today.'

'Then let's leave now,' the captain said.

The next day D'Artagnan arrived in London. He could not speak English so he wrote down the Duke of Buckingham's name on a piece of paper. People soon showed him to the palace. Then a servant took him to the Duke.

At first the Duke did not want to speak to D'Artagnan.

'But I have an important message for you,' D'Artagnan said. 'It is from Queen Anne of France.'

'Anne?' the Duke said. 'What is the message?'

'Last month the Queen gave you a present,' said D'Artagnan. 'She gave you some diamonds. You must give them back to her. There will be a dance next week. The King wants Anne to wear them at the dance.'

Buckingham looked very worried. He was in love with Queen Anne. He did not want her to have problems.

'Come with me,' the Duke said to D'Artagnan. They went together to Buckingham's bedroom. Buckingham opened a box and took out the diamonds. Suddenly, he looked very frightened.

'What's wrong?' D'Artagnan asked.

'There were twelve diamonds,' Buckingham replied. 'But now there are only ten! Someone took them. It must be Cardinal Richelieu's men. He doesn't like me or Queen Anne because we love each other. He wants the King to be angry. It will give Richelieu more power in France.'

'What can we do?' D'Artagnan asked.

'My jeweller will make two more diamonds. Then you must go back to France. You must give the diamonds to the Queen before the dance. The King must not know about this.'

'The diamonds will be ready in two days,' Buckingham went on. 'My jeweller is the fastest and the best in England.'

He was right. Two days later the diamonds were ready.

'Here, D'Artganan, take this note,' the Duke said. He gave D'Artagnan a piece of paper. 'No ships can leave England,' Buckingham told him. 'I gave the order. Go to the port in London. You will find a ship called the *Sund*. Show the captain this note. He will take you to France. Then you must go to an inn with no name. Say the word 'forward' to the innkeeper. He'll give you a horse. There are four more inns like this on the way to Paris. Each innkeeper will give you a horse. You will be in Paris very soon.'

D'Artagnan left with Planchet. Soon he was on a boat called the *Sund*. There were fifty boats on the river. But only the *Sund* could leave. Suddenly D'Artagnan saw a woman on one of the boats. She was very beautiful. But soon he could not see her anymore. He was far out to sea.

# 4

# The Dance and a Meeting

It was the day of the dance and everyone was excited. The palace was full of people and noise. But the King was worried. The Queen looked sad and tired.

Then Cardinal Richelieu spoke to the King quietly. He showed him a box. The box had two diamonds in it. The King started to look angry.

'What is this?' he said.

'You must ask the Queen a question,' said the cardinal. 'Does she still have all twelve diamonds?'

The King walked up to the Queen. 'Madam,' he said. 'Where are the diamonds I gave you? I asked you to wear them at the dance tonight.'

'I'm not wearing the diamonds because I don't want to lose them,' Queen Anne replied.

'But I would like you to wear the diamonds. It will make me very happy,' the King said.

'Then I will wear them,' the Queen replied.

The King and the Queen went to their rooms to get dressed for the dance. But the people saw the King and Queen were not happy. 'What is the problem?' the people asked. 'The King looked very angry.'

Only Cardinal Richelieu looked happy.

The first dance began. The King looked very handsome. The Queen looked beautiful in her diamonds. The King tried to count the diamonds but it was difficult. Then the first dance finished. The King went to the Queen. He showed her the box with the two diamonds.

'Thank you for wearing the diamonds,' he said. 'But two are missing. I've got them here in this box.'

'What do you mean, sir?' the Queen asked. 'Are you giving me two more diamonds? Then I'll have fourteen.'

The King counted the Queen's diamonds. There were twelve on her necklace!

The King and Queen went to find the cardinal. 'My queen is wearing twelve diamonds, not ten,' said the King angrily. 'Why did you give me two more?'

The cardinal looked worried but he thought quickly.

'I gave you two more,' he said, 'because I wanted to give the Queen a present.'

'Thank you, Cardinal,' the Queen replied. She knew the cardinal wanted to make the King angry. But the King was very happy now.

But the happiest person in the palace was D'Artagnan. He knew the Queen was safe because of his trip to England.

'Follow me,' a voice said suddenly. D'Artagnan turned and saw Constance. She took him to a small room.

'I have a present for you,' Constance said. Then she gave D'Artagnan a small ring. He knew it was a present from the Queen. D'Artagnan was very excited, but he wanted something more. He wanted to be with Constance.

'When can I see you again, darling?' he asked.

'Not tonight,' she replied. 'Meet me tomorrow evening. I will see you then. But you must keep it a secret. The address and time are in this letter. Now I must return to the Queen.'

She quickly kissed D'Artagnan and left. D'Artagnan smiled. He was very happy and could not sleep. He thought about Constance all day.

But there was a long time to wait so D'Artagnan decided to look for Athos, Aramis and Porthos. He visited their houses, but they were all empty.

'This is very strange,' D'Artagnan said to himself. 'I'll go and look for them where I left them. But not today. I'll look for them tomorrow. First I must meet Constance.'

D'Artagnan was probably the most excited man in Paris. At nine o'clock he left Paris with Planchet. They rode their horses through the darkness. Constance's note said to meet at St Cloud. St Cloud was a village near Paris. The Queen had a castle there.

D'Artagnan gave Planchet some money. 'You can wait in the inn for me,' he said. 'I'll see you in the morning.'

At the castle, everything was dark. But there was one window with a light in it. D'Artagnan thought it was Constance's window but he could not go into the castle. It was cold outside but D'Artagnan was happy to wait. After half an hour, he heard the clock sound. It was half past ten.

'Constance is late,' he said to himself. 'Or perhaps I'm wrong. Perhaps the meeting is at eleven.'

He took the letter from his pocket and read it again.

*I'll meet you at ten at St Cloud castle.*

D'Artagnan started to feel worried. Where was Constance? Was she asleep or was she in trouble?

It was now eleven o'clock. D'Artagnan could not wait any longer. He tried to climb the wall of the castle, but it was impossible. Then he saw a tall tree next to the lit window. He climbed the tree and looked through the glass. Inside the room was a broken table. There were clothes on the floor. Constance was not in the room.

D'Artagnan came down and looked around the garden. The only thing he found was Constance's glove. Where was she? He ran to a small house by the gate. He knocked on the door and an old man answered.

'Yes sir?' the old man asked.

'I'm looking for my friend,' D'Artagan replied. 'She's a very pretty young woman.'

'There was a pretty woman here earlier this evening,' the man said. 'I can't tell you anything more.'

But D'Artagnan saw that the man knew more. 'Please, tell me,' he said. He gave the man some money.

'Well, all right,' said the man. 'The lady arrived here at about nine o'clock. She went into the castle. Half an hour later, three men arrived. They were dressed like the cardinal's musketeers. They asked me for a ladder. I gave them one. They took the ladder and climbed up to the young lady's window.

They went inside her room. I heard a fight. The lady came to the window and shouted for help. Then they climbed back down with the lady. She looked very frightened.'

D'Artagnan left the old man and went back to the inn. He wanted to look for Constance, but it was impossible. He could not find her in the dark.

# 5

# With Old Friends

The next day D'Artagnan visited Monsieur de Treville. Monsieur de Treville was the captain of the King's musketeers. He was clever and brave. D'Artagnan told him about the men and Constance.

'Hmmm. I think they were the cardinal's men,' Monsieur de Treville said.

'But what can we do?' D'Artagnan asked.

'I know it's very difficult for you, but you must be careful,' Treville replied. 'Those men will probably look for you too. You must leave Paris. I'll tell the Queen about Constance. Go and find Athos, Aramis and Porthos. They will be in danger.'

D'Artagnan thanked the captain. He and Planchet left Paris again. They travelled back to the inn where they left Porthos. D'Artagnan entered the inn. He wore an expensive uniform. He looked rich and important.

'Please have some wine with me,' the innkeeper said. D'Artagnan and the innkeeper started drinking together.

After a short time the innkeeper said,

'I think I know you. I know your face.'

'It's possible,' D'Artagnan said. 'I was here last week with my friends. In fact, I left one of my friends here. His name is Monsieur Porthos. He had an argument with another man about the cardinal.'

'Porthos!' the innkeeper said. 'He is still here.'

'What do you mean?' D'Artagnan asked. 'Is he okay?'

'He's okay. But he is eating all my food and he hasn't got any money,' the innkeeper said.

D'Artagnan went upstairs to see Porthos. Porthos was in bed. He was very happy to see D'Artagnan.

'D'Artagnan, my friend!' he shouted. 'How are you? Is there any news of Athos and Aramis?'

'I don't know where they are. I'm going to look for them now. Come with me,' D'Artagnan said.

'I can't leave here now,' Porthos said.

'Why not?' D'Artagnan asked.

'Because I need money to pay the innkeeper,' Porthos replied. 'I sent a letter to my lover in Paris yesterday, asking for money. I must wait here for her reply.'

D'Artagnan left the inn and rode further. He was happy that Porthos was safe. Now he and Planchet came to the inn where they left Aramis. The innkeeper stood outside.

'Is Monsieur Aramis still here?' they asked her.

'Yes, he is,' she replied. 'But you can't see him.'

'Why not?' D'Artagnan asked.

'He's with two priests,' she said.

D'Artagnan found Aramis' room and entered it. Aramis sat at the table. Two priests sat opposite him.

'Aramis, my friend,' D'Artagnan said. 'Are you ready to come with me? I am going to look for Athos.'

'I'm very sorry, D'Artagnan,' Aramis said. 'But I'm going to be a priest.'

D'Artagnan could not believe it. He did not want Aramis to become a priest. He wanted Aramis to be a musketeer and help find Constance.

'Can I speak to my friend alone, please?' D'Artagnan asked the priests. They did not look very happy, but they left the room. D'Artagnan turned to Aramis.

'Are you sure you want to be a priest, Aramis?' he asked. 'It's a very different life.'

'Ah, I'm very sure, D'Artagnan,' Aramis replied. 'I feel it is the best thing in the world for me.'

'But there is a person who will be sad,' D'Artagnan said. 'They won't be able to meet you anymore.'

'Don't worry,' said Aramis. 'You, Porthos and Athos can meet me.'

'I don't mean us,' D'Artagnan replied. 'I'm talking about Madame de Chevreuse's maid – Mademoiselle Marie Michon.'

D'Artagnan knew that Aramis was in love with Madame de Chevreuse's maid.

'Oh, I'm sure Marie will forget me,' Aramis said. 'She never writes to me now.'

'You are wrong, Aramis,' D'Artagnan said. 'I've got a letter from her here. But of course, you will not want to read it. You're going to be a priest!'

'What are you telling me?' shouted Aramis. 'Here, give me the letter!'

Aramis took the letter from D'Artagnan. It smelled of perfume. Aramis read it quickly. He looked very happy.

'What does it say?' D'Artagnan asked.

'It says that she loves me,' replied Aramis. 'Everything is fantastic!'

'But you're going to be a priest,' D'Artagnan said. 'That means you can't see her.'

'A priest?' Aramis shouted. 'I don't need to be a priest. Love is more important! Let's go and find Athos. Then we'll go back to Paris.'

D'Artagnan felt very happy. Aramis got on his horse and tried to ride. But it was too painful. He was still hurt and he needed to rest.

'Don't worry, Aramis,' D'Artagnan said. 'I'll find Athos and we'll meet you in Paris. You must get better first.'

Aramis agreed. He waved goodbye to D'Artagnan and Planchet.

Soon D'Artagnan and Planchet arrived at the inn. But they could not see Athos or his servant.

'Excuse me, Sir,' said D'Artagnan to the innkeeper. 'What happened to our friend Athos? Do you remember? You told a lie about money. Then three men came. They had a fight with him.'

'Athos?' the man replied. 'Please do not talk about him. It's very bad news.'

'Why? Is he dead?' D'Artagnan asked.

'No, sir, he isn't dead,' the innkeeper replied. 'He was very brave. He killed one of the men and hurt two of them. They ran away. But Athos thinks they will come back. He went into the cellar with his servant to wait for them. And now he's eating all my food and drinking all my wine.'

'Can I speak to him?' D'Artagnan asked.

'You can try,' said the innkeeper.

D'Artagnan knocked on the door to the cellar.

'Who is it?' Athos asked.

'It's me, D'Artagnan.'

'Come in, come in,' Athos shouted. D'Artagnan entered and saw a lot of empty wine bottles.

'Athos, it's so good to see you alive,' D'Artagnan said happily.

'And the same to you, my friend. Did you get to England?' Athos asked.

'Yes, I did,' replied D'Artagnan.

'Then why do you look so sad?' Athos said.

D'Artagnan told Athos about Constance. Athos listened very carefully.

'Love is a terrible business D'Artagnan,' he said at last. 'A terrible business.'

'That's very easy for you to say,' D'Artagnan replied angrily. 'But you're not in love.'

'That's true. I'm not in love,' Athos said. 'But don't be angry with me. I know something about love. A friend of mine was in love once.'

'What happened?' D'Artagnan asked.

'My friend was the lord of a castle,' Athos said. 'A young priest lived in the village near the castle. He lived with his young sister. She was sixteen and very beautiful. No one knew where they came from. It didn't matter. My friend fell in love with the young woman. They decided to get married. He was very stupid.'

'Why was he stupid?' D'Artagnan asked. 'He loved her. That is the most important thing.'

'My friend thought like you,' replied Athos. 'And he was very happy at first. But one day they went riding and his wife fell off her horse. My friend undid her dress to help

28

her breathe. But then he saw something on her shoulder.'

Athos was quiet for a moment. He looked very sad. Then he said, 'On her shoulder she had a mark. The mark is called a "fleur-de-lis". All prisoners in France have this mark. She wasn't the priest's sister. She was an escaped prisoner. In her past she stole a plate from a church.'

'That's terrible!' D'Artagnan said. 'What did your friend do?'

'He killed her. He hanged her on a rope,' Athos said. 'He wanted to hang her brother too, but he escaped. So you see, my friend, sometimes love can be a bad thing.'

D'Artagnan wanted to ask Athos more questions. But Athos did not want to say more.

'Let's have some more wine and food,' he said. 'Then tomorrow we'll go to Paris and look for Constance.'

# 6

# D'Artagnan Meets Milady

The next day the friends arrived in Paris. But there was no time to find Constance. The King was very angry with the English. The English did not like the French. Now, many English ships sailed to France with soldiers. They sailed to a town called La Rochelle.

'We must fight the English at La Rochelle next week,' the French king said to his musketeers.

D'Artagnan and his friends were excited. They liked fighting for the King.

The next day, D'Artagnan and his three friends went to church. In the crowd D'Artagnan saw a beautiful woman. She wore black and she had blonde hair. D'Artagnan could not stop looking at her. Suddenly he remembered her. She was the woman on the boat in London!

D'Artagnan waited for the church meeting to finish. Then he followed the woman home.

The woman lived in a large and beautiful house. D'Artagnan waited outside. Soon he saw the woman's maid leave the house. The maid was young and pretty. She saw D'Artagnan and smiled.

'What is your name?' he asked.

'Kitty,' the maid replied.

'Tell me. Who lives in that large house?' he said.

'My mistress,' Kitty replied. 'She's an English woman. Her name's Milady Clarick.'

'Is she married?' D'Artagnan asked.

'She *was* married,' said Kitty. 'But her husband died. She has a son. Her husband's brother is still alive. His name's Lord de Winter. Milady is in love with the Count de Wardes. I must give him this letter from her.'

D'Artagnan looked at the letter in Kitty's hand. He wanted to meet Milady. He remembered her on the boat. Why was Milady in England?

'Can I see that letter?' he asked Kitty.

'No, sir. It's for the Count de Wardes,' Kitty replied.

'Please,' D'Artagnan said. And because Kitty liked D'Artagnan, she could not say no. D'Artagnan took the letter and read it. The note said,

*I will meet you tomorrow at the Inn of Gold.*

D'Artagnan put the letter in his pocket.

'I would like to meet Madame Clarick,' he said. 'I will go and see her now.' And he went into Milady's house.

D'Artagnan wanted to ask Milady about England. Why was she on a boat there? Did *she* take the diamonds from the Duke of Buckingham?

D'Artagnan soon found Milady but he did not ask her any questions. He could not think. Milady was beautiful and he wanted to be with her. That was all he knew. D'Artagnan said many loving words and Milady was happy to hear them.

D'Artagnan visited Milady every evening. But they only talked. Milady was polite, but she did not love D'Artagnan. She loved the Count de Wardes.

Every night, Milady gave Kitty a letter for the count. But Kitty did not give the letters to the count. She gave the letters to D'Artagnan.

One evening, D'Artagnan wrote a letter back to Milady. The letter said:

*I am sorry I could not see you. I was ill. I will come to your house tomorrow.*

*Count de Wardes*

Kitty gave the letter to Milady. She was very happy. 'Please don't come to my house tomorrow,' she said to D'Artagnan. 'I'll be busy.'

So D'Artagnan did not go to Milady's house. But the

next day, he received a letter from her. The letter said,

*Please visit me tonight. I need your help.*
Milady Clarick

That evening, D'Artagnan visited Milady's house. Milady was very angry. 'Do you love me, D'Artagnan?' she asked him.

D'Artagnan's face was red. 'Yes, I do,' he said.

'Good,' Milady replied. 'And I love you too. But I want you to do something for me. There is a man called the Count de Wardes. He is my enemy. He promised to meet me last night, but he never came. That was very rude. I want you to kill Count de Wardes for me.'

'*Kill* him, Milady?' D'Artagnan asked.

'Yes,' she replied. 'Please, kill him for me. I will love you always.'

D'Artagnan felt surprised and scared. Milady did not know that the letter was from him. She thought it was from de Wardes.

'But I may be hurt,' he said to Milady. 'Or de Wardes may kill me. And then I may never see you again. Please, let me kiss you first.'

Milady did not love D'Artagnan, but she hated de Wardes. So she kissed D'Artagnan. D'Artagnan stayed in Milady's room that night. He was very happy.

The next morning, Milady woke up and said, 'Now you must kill the Count de Wardes.'

D'Artagnan smiled.

'I'm sorry,' he said. 'But I won't kill the count.'

Milady looked surprised. 'What do you mean?' she asked. 'You *must* kill the Count de Wardes. He was very rude to me.'

'No, he wasn't,' D'Artagnan said. 'Now I must tell you the truth. I have all the letters you wrote to de Wardes. He didn't receive them. He didn't write that letter to you. *I* wrote it.'

Milady's face changed. She was suddenly very angry. She tried to hit D'Artagnan, but he caught her hand. Then he saw something on Milady's arm. It was the mark that all prisoners in France receive – the fleur-de-lis.

'You were a prisoner!' D'Artagnan said.

'You lied to me!' Milady shouted. 'And now you know my secret. So you must die!'

D'Artagnan looked down and saw a knife in Milady's hand. He lifted his sword and stepped away from her.

'Don't come near me or I'll kill you,' he shouted. And then he ran out of the house.

D'Artagnan was now Milady's enemy forever.

# 7
# A Trap in La Rochelle

The next day D'Artagnan left for La Rochelle with the other musketeers. But Milady had powerful friends. D'Artagnan was not safe.

Later that day he received a message. It said:

*Please come and see me today. Cardinal Richelieu*

D'Artagnan was very worried. 'I'm in trouble,' he thought to himself.

That evening, he arrived at the cardinal's office. Richelieu smiled at him. D'Artagnan felt very surprised.

'D'Artagnan!' he said. 'I'm very happy to see you.'

'Really, monsieur?' D'Artagnan asked. 'I did not think you knew me.'

'Ah, you are already famous, D'Artagnan,' the cardinal said. 'People say you are the bravest man in France.'

'That's very nice,' D'Artagnan replied. 'But it isn't true. The bravest men in France are my friends: Athos, Aramis and Porthos.'

'Yes, yes, they are brave men too,' replied the cardinal. 'But they are musketeers. They have to be brave.'

'That is true, Cardinal.'

'Do you want to be a musketeer, D'Artagnan?' the cardinal asked.

'Yes, sir. It's my dream,' D'Artagnan replied.

'I would like you to join my musketeers,' Richelieu said. 'Will you fight for me?'

D'Artagnan was very surprised. But he wanted to be a musketeer for the King, not the cardinal.

'Thank you very much, Cardinal,' he said. 'But I'm very sorry. My friends are musketeers for the King. I want to be a musketeer for the King too.'

Now Richelieu looked angry. People never said 'no' to the cardinal!

'Very well, D'Artagnan,' he said. 'But be careful. You have many enemies in Paris.'

D'Artagnan left the cardinal's office. He wanted to tell Athos, Aramis and Porthos about the cardinal's offer. But there was no time. He had to go to La Rochelle to fight the English. Monsieur de Treville needed his help.

D'Artagnan arrived in La Rochelle. There were English soldiers there but no fighting yet. The French soldiers needed to know more about the English soldiers. How good were they? How many guns did they have?

'We need some brave men go to the English camp,' said the French general. 'But it will be very dangerous.'

'I'll go,' D'Artagnan said.

D'Artagnan left an hour later with three other soldiers. They had to be very quiet. They went to look at the English camp. There they saw the English soldiers and their guns. But then the English saw D'Artagnan too. The English shot at D'Artagnan but he escaped with the other soldiers. He was very lucky.

D'Artagnan travelled back to the French camp. There was a present for him there. The present was six bottles of wine. There was a letter with the wine. It said:

*Dear D'Artagnan*
*We are in an inn. We will be in La Rochelle soon. This wine is a present for you.*

*Athos, Aramis and Porthos*

D'Artagnan was very excited. 'Come and have dinner with me!' he said to the other soldiers. He took the wine to the soldiers' kitchen.

D'Artagnan and the soldiers sat at the table. One of the soldiers didn't feel well. D'Artagnan gave him some of the wine.

'Drink this,' he said. 'You'll feel better.'

They watched the soldier drink his wine. Suddenly there was a loud noise.

'It's the war!' D'Artagnan shouted. 'It's started!'

D'Artagnan ran from the room with his sword. He was ready to fight. But the noise was not the war. It was the

sound of the King arriving. Athos, Aramis and Porthos
rode with the King.

'Hello, D'Artagnan!' they shouted.

'Hello,' D'Artagnan said. 'Thank you for the wine.'

'What wine?' Athos asked.

'The wine you sent me.' D'Artagnan replied.

'We didn't send you any wine,' Porthos said.

'But I received six bottles of wine today,' D'Artagnan
said. 'And there was a letter from you.'

'We didn't send a letter to you,' Aramis replied.

Suddenly they heard someone shouting. It was
D'Artagnan's servant, Planchet.

'Come! Help!!' Planchet shouted. D'Artagnan and
the musketeers ran to D'Artagnan's room. There they saw
something terrible. The soldier who drank the wine was
on the floor. He was dead!

'What happened?' D'Artagnan asked.

'He drank the wine, sir,' Planchet replied. 'And then he started to feel very ill.'

Athos took a bottle of the wine. He smelled it.

'This isn't wine,' he said. 'It's poison! Somebody wants to kill you, D'Artagnan.'

'Milady knows I am here,' D'Artagnan said. 'It is war until one of us is dead.'

# 8

# Cardinal Richelieu's Secret Visit

The musketeers waited at La Rochelle, but there was little fighting. Athos, Aramis and Porthos had a lot of free time. One evening they all decided to go to an inn. D'Artagnan was busy and did not go with them.

The three men travelled to the inn on their horses. They drank some wine and then rode back to the soldier's camp. On the way, they met three other men on horses.

It was dark. The musketeers could not see the first man's face. It was covered by a big hat.

'Stop!' Athos shouted to the men. 'Who are you?'

'And who are *you*?' the man with the hat replied.

'What do you mean?' Athos asked. 'Tell me your name or we'll fight you.'

'You will not fight us,' said the man. 'Again, I ask. Who are you?' And then he took his hat off. Athos and the musketeers were very surprised. It was Cardinal Richelieu!

'I'm very sorry, Cardinal,' Athos said. 'My name is Athos. And these are my friends, Aramis and Porthos.'

'Ah, the famous musketeers,' Richelieu said. 'This is very lucky. I am travelling to an inn near here. It's a secret but I need some soldiers for protection. Come with me.'

The musketeers had to follow the cardinal. They rode for five kilometres. They came to the inn and the cardinal went inside with the musketeers.

The cardinal's two men waited outside with the horses.

'Wait in this room for me.' the cardinal said to the musketeers. Then he went upstairs. The musketeers waited.

'What's the cardinal doing?' Aramis asked.

'Listen!' Porthos said. 'I can hear the cardinal talking.'

It was true. The musketeers were in the room below the cardinal. They could hear what he said. They could hear a woman's voice too.

'Milady, I've got an important job for you,' he said.

'*Milady!*' Athos said to himself.

'There is a ship ready for you,' the cardinal said. 'And there are men on the ship who will help you. You must take the ship to England. Go to London and find the Duke of Buckingham. Tell him that I know he's in love with the Queen of France. I've got letters that he sent to her. He must stop the war in France now or I will tell the King. The King will be very angry and Buckingham will never see the Queen again.'

'But he may say no,' Milady said.

'If he says no, you must kill him,' the cardinal replied.

'But that is very dangerous,' Milady said. 'What will you do for me?'

'What do you want?' the cardinal asked.

'I want to find my enemy,' Milady said.

'Who is that?'

'He is called D'Artagnan,' Milady replied. 'You are the most powerful man in France. With your help, I can kill him.'

'Give me a pen and some paper,' the cardinal said. 'I will write a note for you.'

Then the cardinal and Milady stopped talking. The musketeers felt very worried. Milady wanted to kill D'Artagnan. How could they stop her?

'I'm going to leave now,' Athos said.

'But the cardinal will be very angry,' Porthos said.

'Tell him that I'm going to check the road,' Athos replied. 'Don't worry. I've got a plan.'

What was Athos's plan? There was no time to ask. He left the inn quickly.

# 9

# Milady's Secret

'I am going to the forest,' Athos told the cardinal's men. 'I'm going to make it safe for the cardinal.'

Athos got on his horse and rode for a minute. Then he stopped and hid behind some trees. It was dark and nobody could see him. He watched the cardinal and the musketeers leave the inn. They rode their horses back towards the forest. It was dark and soon he could not see them.

Then Athos returned to the inn. He went inside.

'I must give the woman upstairs a message,' he said to the innkeeper. 'It's from the cardinal. Is she in her room?'

'Yes, she is,' the innkeeper replied. 'Go upstairs.'

Athos went upstairs. He looked through the door of Milady's room. She stood in the room with her coat on. Then Athos entered the room. Milady turned and looked at him. Her face turned white with fear.

'You!' she said.

'Yes, that's right, Milady,' Athos said. 'The Count de la Fere. Well, my wife. I thought you were dead. But I see you are still alive.'

'What do you want?' Milady asked him.

'I know you work for the cardinal,' Athos replied. 'You've done many bad things for him.'

'And now I'm going to kill Buckingham,' Milady said.

'That's not important,' Athos said. 'Buckingham is English. But D'Artagnan is my friend. Don't hurt him.'

'D'Artagnan was bad to me,' Milady replied. 'He lied and he hurt me. So I am going to kill him.'

Athos was very angry. He pointed his gun at Milady.

'You will not kill D'Artagnan,' he said. 'And you will give me Cardinal Richelieu's note.'

'I hate you!' Milady shouted. But she could do nothing. Athos had a gun and she did not. She gave him the note. The note said:

*The person who has this note acts for the good of France.*
*Cardinal Richelieu, 5 December 1627*

Athos put the note in his pocket. 'Goodbye, Milady,' he said, and he left the room.

Outside the inn, he found the cardinal's men waiting.

'Take Milady to the ship,' Athos said. 'You must stay with her at all times.'

'Yes, sir,' the men said.

Then Athos got on his horse and rode away. But he did not use the road. He rode his horse through the fields. He arrived at the forest one minute before the cardinal and the musketeers.

'Stop! Who are you?' he shouted at them.

'Athos!' the musketeers shouted. 'It's us, Aramis and Porthos.'

The three musketeers rode to the camp with the cardinal. Aramis and Porthos wanted to ask Athos questions, but it was impossible. The cardinal could hear every word.

Finally, they arrived at the camp. 'Good night, gentlemen,' the cardinal said. 'Thank you for your help.' And then he left.

'Well, what did you do?' Porthos asked.

'Where did you go?' Aramis asked.

'I can't tell you now,' Athos replied. 'First we must find D'Artagnan. We must tell him about Milady.'

A few minutes later, D'Artagnan came to find his friends.

'D'Artagnan,' Athos said, 'I saw Milady.'

'Where did you see her?' D'Artagnan asked. D'Artagnan was brave but he was frightened of Milady.

'She was with Cardinal Richelieu. But don't worry. She is going to England to kill Buckingham.'

'No, Athos,' Aramis said. 'She's going to ask Buckingham to stop the fighting.'

'That is what the cardinal thinks,' Athos replied. 'But Milady wants to kill Buckingham.'

'We must stop her!' D'Artagnan shouted.

'Why?' Athos asked. 'Buckingham is English. France is fighting England. The cardinal gave Milady a note. You should be more worried about that.'

'What note?' D'Artagnan asked.

'This note,' Athos said. He gave it to D'Artagnan. 'I returned to the inn after you left. I took it from Milady.'

He showed his friend Milady's note. D'Artagnan read it quickly.

'What does this mean?' he asked. 'Why did she have it?'

'Because she wants to kill you, D'Artagnan,' Athos replied. 'The cardinal is protecting her.'

'We must kill her first,' Porthos said.

'That's not necessary. She is going to England now,' Athos said. 'She can't hurt D'Artagnan there.'

'But she will kill Buckingham,' D'Artagnan replied. 'I must go to England again and tell him. I like Buckingham. He was good to me.'

'You can't do that,' Athos told him. 'We are at war with England. We were not then. Nobody can go there now.'

'That's true,' Aramis said. 'Perhaps we can write Buckingham a letter.'

'Impossible,' Porthos said. 'We can't write to Buckingham. He's the King's biggest enemy. The letter will never get to England.'

Then D'Artagnan had an idea. 'I know someone who can help us,' he said.

'Who?' the musketeers asked.

'Lord de Winter. Milady doesn't like him and he doesn't like her. He went back to London at the beginning of the war. He'll tell Buckingham about her.'

'That's an excellent idea,' Aramis said.

Soon, Planchet rode his horse from the camp. He was going to the port of Calais. In his pocket was a letter to Lord de Winter.

# 10

# Prison

Milady's journey to England was filled with problems. The weather was very bad and she was five days late. Milady was very angry. She did not want to speak to the Duke of Buckingham. She did not want him to stop the war. She only wanted to kill him.

Finally Milady arrived in England. A soldier waited for her at the ship. The soldier was young and he looked very serious.

'Are you Milady Clarick?' he asked.

'Yes, I am,' she replied.

'I'm here to help you,' he said. Milady did not know the soldier, but he took her bags.

'Please,' the soldier said. 'Follow me.'

Milady followed the soldier to a carriage. But she did not want to get into it.

'I'm fine,' she said. 'Thank you. I will travel to London alone. You don't have to help me.'

'Please get in the carriage,' the soldier replied. 'I won't hurt you. But you must come with me.'

Milady wanted to run, but there were other soldiers near. She could not do anything. She got into the carriage with the soldier.

The carriage left immediately.

'Where are we going?' she asked.

'Don't worry, Milady,' the soldier replied. 'We're going

to a house. You must stay there for a few days. It's because England is fighting France.'

'But that's impossible. Why must I stay in a house? I am English, not French,' Milady shouted.

'I'm sorry, Milady,' the soldier replied. 'I've got my orders. You must go to the house with me.'

Milady was very angry. She had to get out. She had to get to London and find Buckingham. She looked at the door of the carriage. But the soldier saw her.

'Don't jump, Milady,' he said. 'The carriage is moving much too fast.'

Milady could do nothing. She had to sit in the carriage. But the carriage travelled for many hours. Finally, it stopped at a large castle.

'Come with me, please,' the soldier said. He and Milady entered the castle. She followed him to a room. The room was small and comfortable, but there were no windows.

'This is your room, Milady,' the soldier said. 'You must stay here.'

'It's a prison!' Milady shouted. 'Why are you putting me in a prison?'

'Because it is my order,' said a man's voice. Milady looked behind her. Standing there was Lord de Winter, her husband's brother.

'Why are you doing this?' she asked.

'Why are you in England?' Lord de Winter asked.

Milady could not tell him the truth. Lord de Winter was Buckingham's friend.

'I came to see you,' she lied.

'That's very nice,' Lord de Winter said, laughing. 'But I don't believe you. I received a letter yesterday. The letter said something very interesting. Is it true that you want to kill Buckingham?'

Milady felt very angry. She knew the letter was from Athos and the musketeers.

'Of course I don't want to kill Buckingham,' she said. 'Someone is telling lies about me. Please let me go.'

'I'm sorry, Milady,' Lord de Winter replied. 'But I don't believe you. You will stay here for a week or more. Felton will look after you. If you need anything, ask Felton.'

Felton was the name of the young soldier. 'Be careful with her,' de Winter said to him. 'She's the most dangerous woman in England.' And then he left.

# 11

# Escape

The next time Felton came, Milady was on the bed. She looked very ill and Felton was worried.

'Tell Lord de Winter,' he said to a soldier. The soldier found Lord de Winter and brought him to the room. But de Winter looked at Milady and laughed.

'You aren't ill, Milady,' he said. 'Felton, she is lying. Do not believe her.'

Lord de Winter was right. Milady was not ill. She took a knife from the table and tried to kill Lord de Winter! But Lord de Winter laughed again. The knife's end was round and it could not kill anyone.

Lord de Winter left the room. But soon Milady had another plan. She knew that Felton felt sorry for her. The next time he came, she started crying.

'What's wrong?' Felton asked.

'Lord de Winter is very cruel to me,' Milady replied. 'He doesn't like me because I was his brother's wife. He says that I killed his brother. But it's not true. I loved his brother. The Duke of Buckingham killed my husband. He helped Lord de Winter. Lord de Winter wanted his brother's money. If he kills me, he will get all the money.

Felton did not believe her. He left the prison. But the next day, Milady said the same thing. Was it true?

'You know, this is not my first time in prison,' Milady told him.

'What do you mean?' Felton asked.

'I was once in prison before,' she replied. 'But I did nothing wrong.'

'Then why were you in prison?' Felton asked.

'Because Buckingham put me there,' Milady said. Then she started to cry. 'He was in love with me but I didn't love him. He put me in prison and did terrible things to me. My husband was dead and Lord de Winter helped Buckingham. I escaped and now they are scared. They think I'll tell the King.'

'That's terrible,' Felton said. He believed Milady now. He saw she was very beautiful. Everyone knew the Duke of Buckingham liked beautiful women. He was a very powerful man. He could do anything.

At that moment, Lord de Winter came in. He had a letter. It said:

*Take Milady to the ship. If she tries to escape, kill her.*
                                        *The Duke of Buckingham*

'Where are you taking me?' Milady asked.

'That is your choice,' Lord de Winter replied. 'Perhaps America or perhaps Russia. But tomorrow you will leave on a ship.'

Felton and Lord de Winter left together. Milady did not know what to do. How could she escape?

Later that evening Felton woke Milady up.

'Come with me,' he said. 'But you must be quiet.'

'Where are we going? Are you taking me to the ship now?' she asked.

'I'm taking you to *a* ship,' Felton said. 'But not de Winter's ship.'

Milady followed Felton out of the castle. The moon was high in the sky. It was very bright and she could see a ship in the distance. A small boat waited near the beach. Fenton and Milady ran towards it. Soon they were on the ship. Milady was very happy.

'Where is the ship taking us?' she asked Felton.

'It will take you to France. But first we must go to Portsmouth,' Felton replied.

'Why are we going to Portsmouth?' Milady asked.

'Because I'm going to kill Buckingham,' Felton said. 'He will never put you in prison again.'

# 12

# Milady Murders

D'Artagnan and the musketeers were still in La Rochelle. One day, Monsieur de Treville came to visit them.

'Get ready to go to Paris,' he said. 'You leave today.'

'But Monsieur,' Aramis said. 'We cannot leave. We are at war with the English.'

'The war is finished,' Monsieur de Treville said. 'And Buckingham is dead. The English are leaving now.'

Porthos, Aramis and Athos were happy, but D'Artagnan was sad. Buckingham was dead and he knew Milady was the killer.

'Why are you sad?' Monsieur de Treville said. 'I have some very good news for you.'

'What news, sir?' D'Artagnan asked.

'The King has decided to make you a musketeer.'

'Hooray!' the other musketeers said. D'Artagnan felt very proud. It was his dream to be a musketeer. But on the way to Paris, he began to feel unhappy again.

'What's wrong now, my friend?' Athos asked. 'Are you worried about Milady?'

'No,' D'Artagnan replied. 'I'm sad. I still don't know where Constance is. I may never see her again.'

Athos smiled. 'Don't worry,' he said. 'I'm sure you'll see her again.'

And Athos was right. That evening, a letter arrived for Aramis. It was from his cousin. She was one of the Queen's maids. The letter said:

*The Queen's servant, Constance, is hiding in the convent at Béthune. Your friend D'Artagnan can find her there. Please bring her to Paris. It's safe for her now. The Queen wants to see her again.*

Now D'Artagnan was very happy. The musketeers left for Béthune immediately.

Soon after, a letter arrived for the cardinal. It said:

*Buckingham will never leave England again. I'm going to the convent in Béthune. I'll wait for your orders there.*

*Milady Clarick*

The next day Milady arrived at the convent. The nuns in the convent were happy to see her. She told them stories about Paris. One very pretty woman talked to her more than the nuns. This woman was Constance.

'So you are from Paris,' Constance said as they sat together in Milady's room.

'Yes, that's right,' Milady replied.

'Do you know any of the musketeers?' Constance asked.

'Yes, I do,' Milady replied.

'Do you know a musketeer called Athos?' Constance asked with a smile. But she saw Milady's face and stopped smiling. It was white. Milady looked very afraid.

'What's wrong?' Constance asked.

'Nothing,' Milady replied. 'How do you know Athos?'

'He is a friend of D'Artagnan. Do you know D'Artagnan?'

Milady suddenly felt very angry, but happy too. Now she knew who Constance was.

'Are you in love with D'Artagnan?' Milady asked.

'Yes, I am,' Constance replied. 'He's the bravest soldier in France. And he's coming here soon. Look.'

Constance showed Milady a letter. The letter said:

*Your friend D'Artagnan will come for you soon. He is with his friends. Be patient. You will be safe.*

Now Milady was worried. She wanted to kill D'Artagnan but she could not kill him *and* his friends. There were four of them, and only one of her.

There was the noise of horses outside.

'Is it D'Artagnan?' Constance asked.

Milady looked out of the window and shook her head. It was not D'Artagnan and the musketeers. It was Milady's friend, Rochefort. He was the cardinal's best musketeer.

'I'm sorry, but it's not D'Artagnan,' Milady said. 'Stay here. I must go and speak to this man. I'll come back very soon.'

Milady went into the garden of the convent. Rochefort was tall and had a moustache. He smiled at Milady.

'Milady! The cardinal is very happy with you. You did well in England,' he said.

'Yes, but I must leave here now. There is a girl here called Constance. Her lover is D'Artagnan and he's coming here now. I must leave before D'Artagnan and his friends arrive,' Milady said.

'Don't worry. I've got a carriage waiting for you,' Rochford replied. 'The cardinal wants you to come to Paris. I am leaving now so you can follow me.'

'Thank you. I will follow you soon,' Milady said, smiling. 'But I don't want to leave Constance here. First I have to do something.'

Milady returned to her room.

'Who was that?' Constance asked.

'It was my brother,' Milady said. 'But he had some bad news. He said that there are problems in La Rochelle. D'Artagnan and his friends will not come here first. They have to go to Paris.'

'Oh, no!' Constance said. 'I don't want to wait. I want to see D'Artagnan now.'

'Be calm,' Milady said. 'It's not a problem. My brother gave me a carriage. I'm leaving for Paris tonight. You can come with me and meet D'Artagnan there.'

'Oh, thank you!' Constance said.

Constance was very happy. She talked and talked to Milady about D'Artagnan. And Milady listened. Now she had a plan. She did not want to take Constance to Paris. She wanted to kill her too.

But first Milady and Constance had to leave the convent. Milady looked out of the window. The carriage was nearly ready.

'Let's have something to drink before we go,' said Milady. She gave Constance a glass of wine. The two women drank together. Then they heard the sound of horses again. Milady ran to the window.

'Who is it?' asked Constance.

'I don't know,' Milady replied. But then she saw the first rider. It was D'Artagnan. He rode very fast. Behind him rode Athos, Aramis and Porthos.

Milady turned to Constance. 'I don't know these people,' she said. 'They are strangers. You should go to your room. They might be dangerous.'

'I'll go now,' Constance said.

Milady took her glass and filled it with more wine. 'Drink a little more,' she said. 'It will help you relax.'

Constance drank the wine. Then she went to the window and looked down at the men.

'They aren't strangers!' she said to Milady. 'It's D'Artagnan and the musketeers.'

But Milady was no longer in the room.

D'Artagnan was already in the garden. 'Constance! Constance!' he shouted. Constance watched him run to the building.

'I'm here!' she shouted. And soon they were together. D'Artagnan kissed her. Their faces were full of happiness.

'Now we will always be together,' D'Artagnan said.

'Yes, we will,' Constance replied. 'I knew she was wrong. She wanted me to go to Paris with her but...'

'Who is *she*?' D'Artagnan asked.

'The woman who was here,' said Constance. 'Did you see her? She is leaving for Paris.'

'What was her name?' D'Artagnan asked.

'Milady,' Constance replied. 'She was very nice. She knew you and the musketeers. There she is!' Constance pointed out of the window. 'Look! She's in the carriage.'

Suddenly Constance felt very ill. Her face was white and it was difficult to speak. Slowly she fell to the floor.

'Constance!' D'Artagnan shouted. 'What's wrong?'

'I want to sleep now,' Constance replied.

'No, don't sleep,' D'Artagnan said. 'Did Milady give you wine to drink?'

'Yes... she did,' Constance replied. 'Oh, D'Artagnan ... I feel very ill. Please... help me.'

The other musketeers arrived in the room. They saw Constance on the ground. 'What's wrong?' they asked.

'Milady was here,' D'Artagnan replied. 'She gave Constance poison. Quick! We must save Constance.'

'I'm sorry, D'Artagnan,' Athos said. 'But there's nothing we can do. Milady's poison is too strong.'

Athos was right. A minute later Constance was dead.

D'Artagnan held her body and started to cry. At that moment, a young man came through the door. The musketeers turned and looked at him.

'Lord de Winter!' they shouted.

'Hello, gentlemen,' replied Lord de Winter. 'I'm very sorry to see this. I followed Milady from Portsmouth to France. I wanted to catch her but my horse was tired. Now I see I am too late.'

'Yes, you are,' D'Artagnan said. 'Nothing can save my Constance now.' And then he started to cry again.

'My servant Grimaud will follow Milady,' Athos said.

'We must find her and kill her.'

'Yes, you're right,' D'Artagnan shouted. 'Let's find her.'

'But first you must rest,' Aramis said. 'We travelled many miles yesterday. Our horses are very tired. Tomorrow we will find Milady.'

D'Artagnan wanted to leave immediately, but Aramis was right. The horses needed rest. Only Grimaud and the other servants left the convent. The four musketeers and Lord de Winter stayed one more night. They went to bed with thoughts of Milady. They all wanted to kill her.

# 13

## The Truth about Milady

The next morning, Grimaud returned to the convent.

'I followed Milady and I know where she is,' he told D'Artagnan, de Winter and the other musketeers.

'Then we'll go now,' Athos said. And the five men followed Grimaud out of the convent.

The men rode all day. They did not speak. Soon it was night. There was lightning and it started to rain. The five men followed Grimaud to a small house near a river.

Athos went to the house very quietly. There was a small window in the wall. He looked through the window. Milady was alone in the room. She sat in front of the fire. Then one of the horses made a noise. Milady looked up and saw Athos at the window. She ran to the door but she could not escape. D'Artagnan was standing there.

'First we must decide if Milady is guilty,' Athos said. 'So, D'Artagnan, what do you want to say to this woman? Why is she guilty?'

'She is guilty because she killed Constance,' D'Artagnan replied. 'And because she sent poison to me. And because she wanted to kill the Count de Wardes.'

Now Lord de Winter spoke. 'My soldier Felton killed the Duke of Buckingham,' he said. 'Milady told him to do it. And she killed her husband, my brother.'

Finally Athos spoke. 'And she is guilty for one more thing,' he said. 'She has a mark on her shoulder. It was the mark of a prisoner – the fleur-de-lis. I tried to kill her but she escaped. Porthos and Aramis, what do you think? Is Milady innocent or guilty? What should we do?'

Milady started to cry. 'I don't want to die! I don't want to die!' she shouted. But the musketeers caught her arms and took her from the house. Suddenly Milady tried to escape. She ran for fifty metres but then she fell. Soon the musketeers caught her. It was now very dark. They were next to a river.

Athos stood above her and took out his sword.

'I pardon you for what you did,' he said. 'Die in peace.'

'I pardon you for what you did,' said de Winter.

'I pardon you for what you did,' said D'Artagnan.

Then Athos dropped the sword and Milady was dead.

## 14

# The Cardinal and D'Artagnan

Three days later the four friends returned to Paris. That evening, Rochefort arrived.

'D'Artagnan,' Rochefort said. 'You must come with me. The cardinal wants to see you.'

D'Artagnan followed Rochefort to the cardinal's office. He felt nervous. Then he saw the cardinal and felt more nervous. The cardinal was very angry.

'D'Artagnan,' he said. 'You are an enemy of France. You travelled to England and met Buckingham. You wrote to him during the war...'

'Who said this?' D'Artagnan asked. 'Was it Milady?'

'Yes, it was,' the cardinal said. 'She is my best spy.'

'Do not believe Milady. She is a liar and a murderer,' D'Artagnan replied. 'She married one man in France and another man in England. She killed my lover Constance. And she killed her husband. She was a prisoner but she escaped. She had the fleur-de-lis on her arm.'

'This isn't true,' the cardinal said.

'It is true, sir,' replied D'Artagnan.

'Then I'll ask Milady about it.'

'Milady is dead sir,' said D'Artagnan.

Cardinal Richelieu looked very shocked. 'Dead?' he asked. 'Who killed her?'

'I killed her,' D'Artagnan replied. 'But look, sir. I have your note of permission in my pocket.'

He gave the cardinal the piece of paper.

*The person who has this note acts for the good of France.*
*Cardinal Richelieu, 5 December 1627*

D'Artagnan watched the cardinal read the note. Slowly his face changed. He knew D'Artagnan was right. With the letter, D'Artagnan could kill anyone.

The cardinal wrote something on a piece of paper. Then he gave it to D'Artagnan.

'Here,' he said. 'Take this. There is no name on the paper, but it can be your name.'

D'Artagnan did not understand. He looked at the paper. The paper said:

_____ *will be a lieutenant of the King's* *musketeers.*

*Cardinal Richelieu*

'But I cannot be a lieutenant,' D'Artagnan said.

'Yes, you can,' the cardinal replied. 'You are very brave. You don't have to be a lieutenant. You can give the paper to a friend. But I want you to be a lieutenant in the King's musketeers. Please think about it.'

'Yes, sir,' D'Artagnan said.

Later that evening he saw Athos. He showed him the paper.

'Athos,' D'Artagnan said. 'You are a better musketeer than me. You must be a lieutenant.'

'Thank you, D'Artagnan,' Athos replied. 'But I can't be a lieutenant. I'm leaving the musketeers. I want to live as the Count de la Fere again. Good luck.'

The next person D'Artagnan saw was Porthos. D'Artagnan showed him the paper.

'Porthos,' D'Artagnan said. 'You are a better musketeer than me. You must be a lieutenant.'

'Thank you, D'Artagnan,' Porthos replied. 'But I'm leaving the musketeers. I'm going to marry my lover.'

There was one more musketeer. D'Artagnan found Aramis in a church.

'Aramis,' he said. 'You are a better musketeer than me. You must be a lieutenant.'

'Thank you, D'Artagnan,' Aramis replied. 'But I can't be a lieutenant. I'm leaving the musketeers. I'm going to become a priest. This time I am sure.'

D'Artagnan returned to Athos's house. 'Nobody wants to be a lieutenant,' he said to Athos. 'They all said "no".'

'That's because you are the best musketeer,' Athos replied. 'You must be the lieutenant.'

Then Athos took the paper and wrote D'Artagnan's name in the space.

'But I'll have no friends,' D'Artagnan said. 'You are leaving. Porthos is getting married and Aramis is going to be a priest. And Constance is dead.'

But Athos looked at D'Artagnan and smiled.

'My friend,' he said. 'You are young. You are sad now, but be patient. In the future, you will be very happy again. I promise you.'

And Athos was right.

# Exercises

## People in the story

The following characters are in the story. Write a name next to a description below. The first one is done for you.

D'Artagnan   Athos   Aramis   Porthos   Constance   Milady
Cardinal Richelieu   Rochefort   The Duke of Buckingham
~~Queen Anne~~   The King   Lord de Winter   Planchet

| 1 | Queen Anne | The King's wife and the lover of the Duke of Buckingham. |
|---|---|---|
| 2 | | Is in love with Constance and wants to be a King's musketeer. |
| 3 | | An escaped prisoner, who poisons Constance. |
| 4 | | A musketeer who was married to Milady and tried to kill her. |
| 5 | | D'Artagnan's servant. |
| 6 | | The Queen's maid, who is in love with D'Artagnan. |
| 7 | | The other powerful frenchman who also has special musketeers. |
| 8 | | Anne's husband, who gave her diamonds. |
| 9 | | The brother of Milady's husband. |
| 10 | | A rich English man who is Anne's lover and is killed. |
| 11 | | One of the musketeers, who becomes a priest at the end of the story. |
| 12 | | One of the musketeers, who is going to marry his lover at the end of the story. |
| 13 | | Milady's friend and the cardinal's best musketeer. |

# Multiple choice

**Tick the best answer.**

1 Why did D'Artagnan go to England?
   - **a** To fight the English
   - **b** To find Constance
   - **c** To get the Queen's diamonds  ✓
   - **d** To stop Milady killing Buckingham

2 Who took Constance from the castle in St Cloud one night?
   - **a** D'Artagnan
   - **b** The three musketeers
   - **c** The cardinal's men
   - **d** Milady

3 Why did Milady want to kill D'Artagnan?
   - **a** Because he stole money from her
   - **b** Because he was French and she was English
   - **c** Because he lied to her and knew she was a prisoner
   - **d** Because he wanted to be a musketeer for the King, not the cardinal

4 Who died from poisoned wine?
   - **a** Constance only
   - **b** Constance and D'Artagnan
   - **c** Constance and a soldier
   - **d** Constance and Milady

5 Who killed Milady and how?
   - **a** D'Artagnan with a gun
   - **b** Athos with a sword
   - **c** D'Artagnan with poison
   - **d** Athos with a knife

6 Who became a lieutenant of the King's musketeers?
   - **a** Athos
   - **b** Porthos
   - **c** Aramis
   - **d** D'Artagnan

# The author

**Choose the correct information to complete the sentences.**

1  The author Alexandre Dumas was <u>English</u> / <u>(French.)</u>

2  Dumas <u>went</u> / <u>did not go</u> to school.

3  Dumas wrote <u>modern</u> / <u>historical</u> plays and books.

4  Dumas's <u>son</u> / <u>daughter</u> was also a writer.

5  Dumas also lived in <u>Russia</u> / <u>Spain</u>.

6  Dumas died in <u>1802</u> / <u>1870</u>.

# Vocabulary: people

**There are many nouns in the story which are types of people. Complete the gaps with letters to make a word which is a type of person. The first one is done for you.**

1  The opposite of a friend is an e <u>n</u> <u>e</u> <u>m</u> y.

2  Someone who does something wrong and goes to prison is a p _ _ _ _ _ _ r.

3  A person whose job is to fight in a war is a s _ _ _ _ _ r.

4  A person who makes rings and necklaces is a j _ _ _ _ _ _ r.

5  A person who steals is a t _ _ _ f.

6  A person who worked for a rich person in their home was a s _ _ _ _ _ t.

7  An important person in the (Catholic) church is a p _ _ _ _ t.

8  A person who is in love with another but is not married to them is their l _ _ _ r.

9  A person who does not tell the truth is a l _ _ r.

10  A person who kills another is a m _ _ _ _ _ _ r.

# Grammar: superlatives and comparatives

Complete the sentences with either the superlative form (eg *most* +
adjective / adjective + *-est*) or comparative form (eg *more* + adjective /
adjective + *-er*) of the adjective in brackets. The first two questions are
examples.

1   Athos said that D'Artagnan was a ........*better*........ (good)
musketeer than him.

2   The King was the ........*richest*........ (rich) man in France.

3   Buckingham's jeweller was the ........................ (fast) and
........................ (good) jeweller in all of England.

4   D'Artagnan was the ........................ (excited) man in Paris on
the evening that he was going to meet Constance at St Cloud.

5   Only the very ........................ (brave) soldiers could be the King's
musketeers.

6   When D'Artagnan knew the truth about Milady, he understood that
Constance was ........................ (nice) and ........................
(beautiful) than her.

7   Milady told the cardinal that he was the ........................
(powerful) man in all of France, even ........................ (powerful)
than the King.

8   Going to look at the English camp during the war was one of the
........................ (dangerous) things that the general could ask
D'Artagnan to do.

9   After helping the Queen by bringing her the diamonds, D'Artagnan
was the ........................ (happy) person in the palace.

10  Aramis will probably have a ........................ (quiet) life as a
priest than as a musketeer.

11  Porthos told the traveller that the King was a ........................
(good) man than the cardinal.

12  It was ........................ (dangerous) for D'Artagnan to go to
England than for him to stay in France.

# Vocabulary: verbs + nouns

Match a verb and noun together to make an expression from the story. The first one is done for you.

| | | | |
|---|---|---|---|
| 1 | get on | | a gun |
| 2 | tell | | a question |
| 3 | point | | a horse |
| 4 | climb | | diamonds |
| 5 | ask | | the bill |
| 6 | wear | | a lie |
| 7 | pay | | prison |
| 8 | escape from | | a tree |

# Vocabulary: adjectives to describe feelings

Choose the best adjective to describe how the characters felt in the story.

1 D'Artagnan feels (nervous) / angry / happy / excited when Cardinal Richelieu calls him to his office. He does not know what the cardinal is going to say, but it is probably bad news.

2 Cardinal Richelieu knows that the King will be angry / impatient / frightened / nervous if he learns that the Queen gave the diamonds to her lover.

3 D'Artagnan is frightened / happy / surprised / angry that the Queen can wear the diamonds at the dance.

4 Milady suddenly becomes very frightened / angry / happy / excited when D'Artagnan tells her that her lover did not receive the letters she wrote to him.

5 Constance was excited / frightened / impatient / sad when the cardinal's men took her from the castle at night.

6   D'Artagnan was <u>angry / worried / sad / happy</u> when Constance was not at the castle at 10pm to meet him – he thought something was wrong.

7   D'Artagnan was <u>scared / impatient / happy / excited</u> when Milady asked him to kill the Count de Wardes.

8   When Milady's journey to England became five days late because of bad weather, she was very <u>nervous / happy / impatient / scared.</u>

## Making questions

**Look at the example, then use question words (*who/why/what/where/ when/how*, etc) to complete the questions for the answers shown.**

> **Example:** *Who* wrote *The Three Musketeers?*
> Alexandre Dumas wrote *The Three Musketeers.*

Q1   ........................ does the story happen?
A1   In 1625.

Q2   ........................ country is D'Artagnan from?
A2   France.

Q3   ........................ many diamonds does Cardinal Richelieu show the King?
A3   Cardinal Richelieu shows the King two diamonds.

Q4   ........................ does the soldier die?
A4   The soldier dies because he drinks poison.

Q5   ........................ do the French fight the English?
A5   At La Rochelle.

Q6   ........................ does the Queen give D'Artagnan as a present?
A6   A ring.

Q7   ........................ brother is Lord de Winter?
A7   Lord de Winter is Milady's husband's brother.

Q8   ........................ long does Porthos stay at the inn?
A8   He stays there for a week.

Published by Macmillan Heinemann ELT
Between Towns Road, Oxford OX4 3PP
A division of Macmillan Publishers Limited
Companies and representatives throughout the world
Heinemann is the registered trademark of Pearson Education, used under licence.

ISBN 978–0–2307–3115–8
ISBN 978–0–2307–1673–5 (with CD edition)

This version of *The Three Musketeers* by Alexandre Dumas was retold by
Nicholas Murgatroyd for Macmillan Readers

First published 2009
Text © Macmillan Publishers Limited 2009
Design and illustration © Macmillan Publishers Limited 2009
This version first published 2009

Illustrated by David McAllister and Martin Sanders
Cover photograph by Rex Features/SNAP

Printed and bound in Thailand
2012 2011 2010
7 6 5 4 3

with CD edition
2012 2011 2010
7 6 5 4 3